This Little Tiger book belongs to:

For Jude and Barry, with love - T C x

For my little nephew, Isaac - T W x

LITTLE TIGER PRESS
1 The Coda Centre,
189 Munster Road, London SW6 6AW
www.littletiger.co.uk

First published in Great Britain 2016
This edition published 2016

Visit Tim Warnes at www.ChapmanandWarnes.com

A CIP catalogue record for this book is available from the British Library

ISBN 978-1-84869-266-4
LTP/1400/1438/0216
Printed in China
2 4 6 8 10 9 7 5 3 1

NOW!

Tracey Corderoy

Tim Warnes

LITTLE TIGER PRESS
London

Archie found waiting
a little bit hard.

He wanted to have all the fun **NOW!**

HH!
Wait, Archie!
TOO MUCH!

Each day was full of exciting things.

And when did Archie want them . . . ?

NOW!
Archie

NOW!
Bouncy Castle
Queue here!

But even Archie had to agree that **"NOW!"** wasn't always best . . .

Let's stick it up
NOW!
Are you sure
it's dry?

Plip!
Plop!
SPLAT!
Waaaaa!

To help Archie wait they made a count-down chart. Dad used his special pens.

They played aeroplanes too . . .

and made a jumbo jet model.

As Archie crossed off the days, he got more and more excited . . .

Very nearly now?
Getting closer. . .

Very, VERY nearly now??
Yes! Just one more sleep!

They searched **EVERYWHERE**.

Mum and Dad checked the clock.
"We'll miss the plane!" they gasped.

They whisked Archie into the car.

And guess who

was there . . .

TIGER!

"Ahh, thank goodness!" said Mum. And off they went.

DEPARTURES
At the airport,
the queue was
ENORMOUS.
But Archie was
very, very patient.
Check-in
Please have your
tickets ready.
Good boy!

At last, they fastened their seatbelts.

And – **zooooom!**

– up went the plane.

"Was it worth the wait then, Archie?" asked Dad.

But all Archie could say **now** was . . .

WOW!

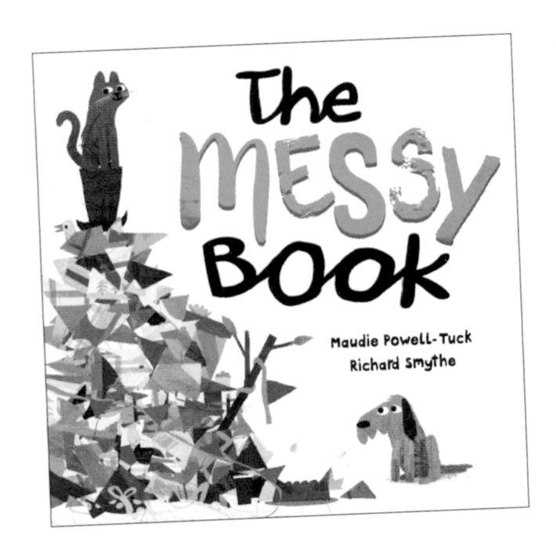

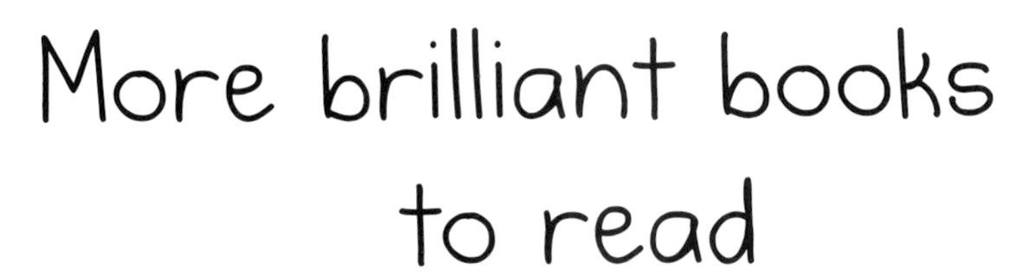

NOW!

For information regarding any of the above titles
or for our catalogue, please contact us:
Little Tiger Press, 1 The Coda Centre,
189 Munster Road, London SW6 6AW
Tel: 020 7385 6333
E-mail: contact@littletiger.co.uk
www.littletiger.co.uk